D0520445

# It's Monday, Mrs. Jolly Bones!

Warren Hanson
illustrated by Tricia Tusa

BEACH LANE BOOKS

New York London Toronto Sydney New Delhi

For Rebecca Joy, the real Mrs. Jolly Bones—W. H.
For who else but Ms. Caroline "Jolly Bones" Martin—T. T.

BEACH LANE BOOKS
An imprint of Simon & Schuster Children's Publishing Division
1230 Avenue of the Americas, New York, New York 10020
Text copyright © 2013 by Warren Hanson
Illustrations copyright © 2013 by Tricia Tusa
All rights reserved, including the right of reproduction in whole or in part in any form.
BEACH LANE BOOKS is a trademark of Simon & Schuster, Inc.
For information about special discounts for bulk purchases, please contact Simon & Schuster Special Sales at
1-866-506-1949 or business@simonandschuster.com.
The Simon & Schuster Speakers Bureau can bring authors to your live event. For more information or to book an event,
contact the Simon & Schuster Speakers Bureau at 1-866-248-3049 or visit our website at www.simonspeakers.com.
Book design by Debra Sfetsios-Conover
The text for this book is set in Grit Primer.
The illustrations for this book are rendered in watercolor and ink.
Manufactured in China
1212 SCP
First Edition
10 9 8 7 6 5 4 3 2 1
Library of Congress Cataloging-in-Publication Data
Hanson, Warren.
It's Monday, Mrs. Jolly Bones! / Warren Hanson ; illustrated by Tricia Tusa.—1st ed.
p. cm.
Summary: Mrs. Jolly Bones goes through the week, doing chores in her unique way.
ISBN 978-1-4424-1229-3 (hardcover)
ISBN 978-1-4424-3621-3 (eBook)
[1. Stories in rhyme. 2. Housekeeping—Fiction. 3. Week—Fiction. 4. Humorous stories.]
I. Tusa, Tricia, ill. II. Title. III. Title: It is Monday, Mrs. Jolly Bones!
PZ8.3.H19655It 2013
[E]—dc22
2010004309

It's Monday, Mrs. Jolly Bones.
There's laundry to be done.

So gather up the dirty clothes
and sort them, one by one.

Wash them,

dry them,

iron them,

and fold them nice and neat.
Then fling them out the window...

so they brighten up the street!

It's Tuesday, Mrs. Jolly Bones. There's gardening to do.
The peas and beans need weeding, and the squash need water too.
Now hoe those rows of onions. Keep the cornstalks growing high.

Then polka through the posy patch and make those flowers fly!

It's Wednesday, Mrs. Jolly Bones. It's time to clean the house.
So wear your worn-out overalls. Put on your oldest blouse.
Sweep all the floors, shake all the rugs, and shine the sink and tub.

Then step into the toilet bowl and give yourself a scrub!

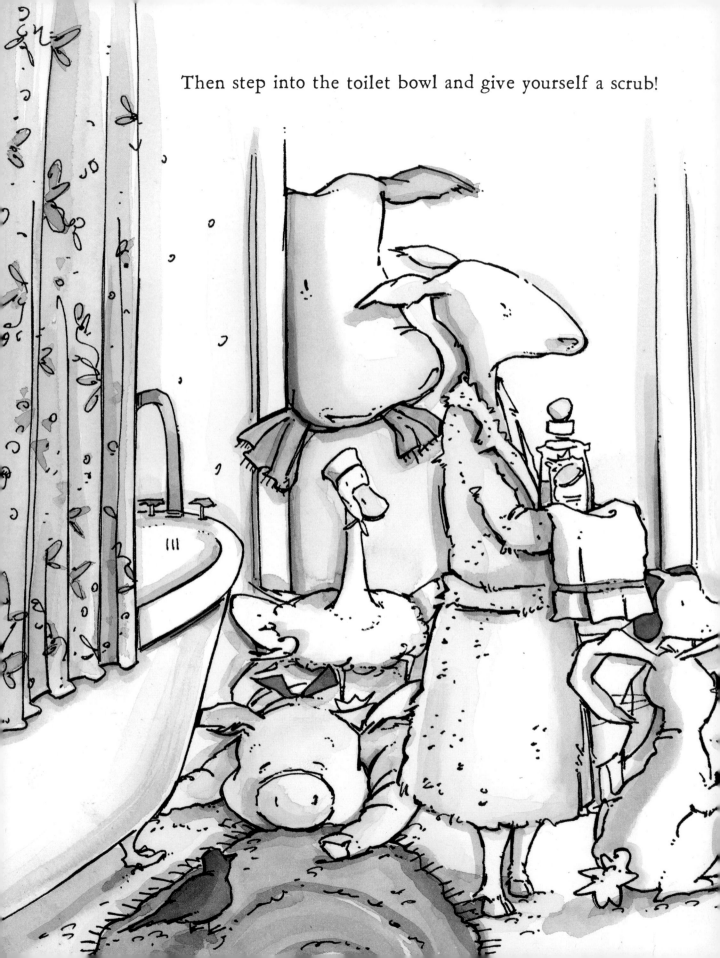

It's Thursday, Mrs. Jolly Bones.
The cupboard's getting bare.

You must get to the market.
There are suppers to prepare.

Get peanut butter, pickled herring, prunes, and sausage links.

Then cook them all in cabbage juice until the kitchen stinks!

It's Friday, Mrs. Jolly Bones.
A perfect day to bake.

Get flour, sugar, milk, and eggs, and make a birthday cake!
Add lovely decorations—little roses would be nice.

Then fire up the power saw
and cut yourself a slice!

It's Saturday, a day for Mrs. Jolly Bones to play.
The food and clothes and tools and brooms have all been put away.

Invite the ladies over.

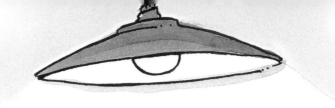

Share some gossip and some tea.

Then clear away the furniture . . .

and wrestle recklessly!

It's Sunday, Mrs. Jolly Bones. A day for you to rest.
Put pillows all around yourself and make a cozy nest.
Enjoy a glass of buttermilk, a cookie, and a nap.

Then yodel until midnight with a chicken in your lap!

You did it, Mrs. Jolly Bones! You finished up your week.
You did your daily chores, and with a style that's quite unique!

But when tomorrow morning comes, oh, what will you do then?

It's Monday, Mrs. Jolly Bones—
let's do it all again!